DEEP WATER AND OTHER STORIES

DEEP WATER AND OTHER STORIES

KATHRYN TRATTNER

ISBN: 9781677784066

First printing, 2020

www.kathryntrattner.com

for the ones I love the most

Driven by the forces of love, the fragments of the world seek each other so that the world may come into being.

PIERRE TIEHARD DE CHARDIN

CONTENTS

1

BATTLEFIELD MUSE

EACH BLAST SEPARATE, unique, the bombs falling from the sky and getting nearer. After months at the front, Sam could tell roughly where they'd land, how far from him they'd be. He ducked, dirt pattering down, plunking on his helmet, dusting his shoulders. He didn't bother brushing it away.

At first he'd covered his ears, hunched his shoulders, pulled his head in like a turtle. Not now. The man beside him coughed, hacking blood. He'd been too slow with his mask the last time they'd been gassed. But he hadn't told the commanding officer. The man wanted to stay, half buried in the earth, sweating and bleeding and dying by inches in the trenches.

Sam touched his pocket, felt the wad of paper there, the comfort of civilization when nothing else appeared sane. The words were a lifeline, a rope, to a world that he'd forgotten. He knew, he had to believe, that it remained, past the machine gun nests and the field hospital, away on the hazed horizon.

His belief alone would make it real.

He fumbled the packet free, digging out the stub of a pencil he'd kept, whittled, and preserved.

He began to write.

They wrote the poetry of the war and I collected it. Going from man to man, taking pages, rustling, clutching them to my chest as explosions rattled my bones.

In all those faces there was one—as there always is, as there always has to be. I pressed my lips to his eyes, expecting to give him sight. But he couldn't see me and his well of sorrow that overflowed dropped me to my knees.

In a moment they would launch themselves, breath and bone, soul and tender heart, over the lip of the trench and into barbed wire hell. The bombardments had come to a halt, the silence in their wake eerie, expectant.

I watched him scribble a few last words on a scrap of paper. The pencil blunt, the pages greasy. The words were almost unintelligible, blurred and run together with haste and the shaking hand of adrenaline. I crouched, the hem of my nurse's uniform sinking into mud without being stained by it. I brought my face to his, looking past the layer of grime, through tanned flesh to the mind twinkling behind bone. He sparked, he shone, his verse coming from a place I couldn't go. I hadn't touched him, hadn't made a gift of my services, and still he wrote.

Down the line, past bent helmeted heads and rifles topped with bayonets, a man with Captain's bars stood, smoking. His hand remained steady, his eyes squinting at an unseen point. Then he called it, ordering them to stand, the boys and men, the soldiers dressed in khaki. A rattle of gear, right to left, past my line of sight, they moved, becoming one being.

My poet slipped the packet of pages into his breast pocket, careful to button it closed. I eased my hand in, took the sheets so that they wouldn't be lost. Mine leaving just as his came up to pat the spot, keeping the small piece of heart he carried outside of his body safe.

I did this each time. I took the words he carried into battle, fearful that he would fall and they'd be lost. I couldn't bear the thought that our eyes would be the only ones to see his work, to absorb the greatness in simple lead. Each time he came back I replaced them, breathing out a sigh that wasn't quite relief—who am I to feel such things? A muse, the flash of inspiration, nothing substantial.

But this time, *this time*, it felt different. The air smoked and steamed, hot with anticipation, the fetid mess at the bottom of the trench, knee-deep in places, crawling after the soldiers as they rushed over the top and into enemy fire.

I followed, not onto the field, but to the lip so that I could watch their progress, see the bodies fall. Bullets whizzed, whining through me, past my cheekbones, through my gut, but I remained, silent and ever watchful.

Death and I, we were friends in those days—much closer than we are now. He came to stand beside me, leaning on the silver bayonet-topped rifle he'd fashioned, leaving the traditional scythe at home.

"One of yours?" He nodded at the advancing line, the men crouched, ducking shells and fire, the world coming apart.

I shook my head, unable to look away for fear I would lose sight of him and in that instant he'd take his last breath.

Death snorted, "Why watch, then?"

"He writes beautiful poetry." I held the smudged pages aloft.

"Let me see." Death took them, the sting of it leaving my hand, reaching all the way to my soul.

He flipped through the little packet, mumbling as he skimmed, one finger tapping against the rifle. He shrugged, or I imagined he did, because I didn't look at him. "It's good. And you didn't help?"

"No."

"How often does that happen?"

"A natural?"

"Yes."

"Never."

"Maybe he's someone else's then. Seen any of the others floating around the place?"

Out of the corner of my eye, Death leaned forward, glancing left and right, up and down, as if he might catch sight of another on the battlefield.

"Not lately," I said, hand going to my mouth. My poet had fallen, tripping over a body, a shell exploding close, too close. He didn't move. I started forward.

Death stopped me, a hand on my arm, his cold infecting me. "He's fine. He'll get up in a minute."

I waited, watching, until he did and then I let myself breathe. Death tapped me with the packet of pages; I accepted them, clutching them to my chest as if by saving them I could save the flesh marching across the field.

"I could tell you," Death leaned closer, tilting his voice at me, creeping up on me, "you know, when it's going to happen. Might take some of the worry away, the wait."

I shook my head, "I don't want to know."

"You're sure?"

I nodded.

The battle raged. I'd never understood that term, a battle raging, as if this experience had a life and anger and fury all its own. But here, watching, the world around me imploding only to expand in a shower of mud, blood, and shrapnel, it felt as if the earth had coughed up all the hate and malice, the anger and fury that a universe could hold and unleashed on the little figures rushing across the surface. It was hard to believe that man could choose this, could hunch in trenches and wait for the call, to go over the top and run screaming at each other.

"You're really sure?"

I turned to Death, wrenching my gaze away to stare into his pale face. He smiled at me a little sadly, as if he pitied me, or as if he knew I'd be taking on a weight I couldn't carry.

"I'm sorry," he said, not unkindly but business like, reaching out to pat my shoulder. I pushed his hand away, turning back to the field. It had changed, just in that instant, my poet, my rushing heart disappeared.

"Why did you do that?" I searched the spot where I'd last seen the man, but he was gone. A crater, larger than the rest, dirt still falling, occupied that space. I balled my hands into fists, "Why?"

"No one should have to watch someone they love die."

I ran, stumbling for an instant in rutted earth until I willed myself above it, my feet barely touching the ground as I propelled myself forward. I leapt, brushing a jangling barbed wire fence, floating over fallen soldiers. I passed through them, they passed through me, until I found the one I sought. Several yards from the crater, mangled and broken, his skin so pale it was almost blue. His face was turned to the overcast ceiling of the world, the sky above lit with flashing and popping explosions.

I knelt beside him, touched my lips to his temple, tasted blood. He couldn't see me, would not. In my hand his pages rustled, a song for the dead, the dying, and gone. I held them tighter, promised life, the only kind I could give.

"He was young." Death was there, bayonet at the ready, sharp silver point reflecting some other place than this. "Ready?"

I nodded, reaching out to take the poet's hand. Not that he would feel it or care but to comfort myself, to feel the weight of this a little less.

Death plunged the bayonet into the ruin of his chest, cutting his soul lose, freeing it for what came next. There was an instant, an almost, a shade, then nothing. I was left with the cooling body, bloodied uniform, and Death with his clean bayonet. I looked around, deaf to the screaming, the crying. None of them belonged to me.

"You've got a lot of work," I said, letting the poet's hand drop, pushing to my feet. I brushed a hand against the white cotton of my dress, smearing blood and dirt across it.

Death nodded, glanced around. "I do. No rest for the wicked, as they say."

I smiled, weakly, tentative because my face hurt from holding back tears. "Better get to it."

He spun his rifle like a trained cadet, shouldering it as if he intended to march off to some private battle of his own. I didn't stay to watch him spear the rest, to collect them, to move them on.

I walked away, stepped off the field, leaving the sounds of it behind me. I walked until I could no longer smell the decay, the muddy feces and fear.

I walked until around me a city blossomed, shooting

great stone stalks out of the earth, stained glass petals shimmering.

I found a place where I could wait out time.

Later, oh so many years later, I discovered a poet I liked. He wasn't as good as the natural, his talent needed something, a push that he couldn't give himself. In a café, surrounded by excited voices, ideals and art, unseen I whispered him my natural's words. I read them into his ear so that no else might hear.

I made my voice the music of loved pages, worn words.

Ink flowed, words appearing across the new paper in a bold strong hand. I smiled when I saw his lips move, smiled as he read them aloud and marveled that he could write something so striking.

2

THE GOLDEN NIGHT

A ROLLS-ROYCE COLLECTED ME, gold, trimmed in chrome and upholstered in velvet with a smoked glass partition between my seat and the chauffeur. I'd never ridden in one, never seen one though I'd heard the name. I sat, gliding down the road, wrapped in a dream of steel and rubber.

Gravel crunched beneath the tires and, through the windows, tall trees rushed by, upright and hunter green in the night. They blurred, merging, morphing into a wall. They looked like pine or spruce and I imagined the sharp scent of sap. But, in the closed cab, my perfume was overwhelming.

It had all come from him; the dress of bright beaded sunrise, the expensive bottle of scent, the stockings, the shoes. A box had arrived two hours before the car, plain white, no ribbon, no card. The tissue paper had been fresh as driven snow. I had thought he would be more extravagant, that his flair would have come through in the wrapping. But the dress had made up for the plainness and, seeing the detailing and silk, I found myself thankful for the white box and unwrinkled tissue.

I wore gold tonight, becoming spark or flame, a lighted window facing darkness. I matched the car, all glitter and chrome, encased in gold stockings and dancing shoes. He'd picked a shade that set off the warm tones in my ordinary brown hair, in my run-of-the-mill dark eyes. Reflected in the bathroom mirror had been a woman I'd never seen before, her smile one I didn't know.

The car slowed, following the curve of a circular drive before a great pale house. My stomach clenched. The house was dark, seemingly empty, shut tight against visitors and ghosts. I thought the car might continue, that we'd sweep past the house and back down the long tunnel of the drive, where the trees would bend to pluck at my dress, to pull the feather from my hair.

But no; the car stopped, rumbling, purring in satisfaction. I hesitated, wondering if the chauffeur would open my door. He remained seated, head forward. My palms were slick with sweat, my armpits prickled. I sucked in a breath for calm. Screwing up my courage, I fumbled with the door latch and pushed it open. I stepped out, shutting the door behind me. The car pulled away before I heard the latch click.

Alone, I looked up at the house. The muggy summer air mouthed my skin, collecting in the hollow of my collar bone, slipping beneath the silk of my slip to run sticky fingers over my thighs.

I went up the wide front steps to the brass knocker gleaming in the light of the moon, and I knocked. A ripple of unease at the night, at the hushing of wind through trees, the silence of the facade, tickled across my neck, raising hairs.

I nervously bunched the dress in my hand, feeling the

bite of beadwork, rumpling perfection. I forced myself to let it go, to relax.

The door swung open, a little sun exploding and engulfing me. Monroe was there. I smelled the tobacco of the cigar clamped between his teeth, felt his hands before I saw him. I found his eyes, smiling, as he ushered me inside.

Live music assailed me, so loud I put my hands to my ears. A thumping, swinging jazz, the smoke of the singer's voice something almost solid that I inhaled with each breath I took. From the outside, the place had been forlorn, abandoned, but inside a thousand voices filled the space. Monroe eased me through a crowd of so many people that they obscured the artwork on the walls. The high ceilings gathered curled cigarette smoke.

He had not spoken yet—it was too noisy, other people's conversations too intrusive. He took me to a corner in a wide sitting room, the back wall all leaded glass windows looking onto the lawn. Even here, he pressed his mouth to my ear to be heard.

"I'm so glad you came."

I nodded, glancing at him, an inner shiver of delight too much to take.

"You *are* so lovely."

I smiled, fingering the dress, touching his shoulder and standing on my toes until my lips brushed his ear. "Thank you for the dress."

He smiled, surveying the room and his guests. I wondered how he knew so many people or if, in the way of such events, they had arrived without invitation or knowledge of the host, to drink gin and dance. He didn't seem to mind.

He mimed getting a drink; I nodded, and he snaked away. I watched as a guest stopped him, voices raised to carry on a conversation. I admired the cut of his white tuxedo, marveling that he kept it so clean. The partygoers wore their finery, black tie and pearls, filmy transparent gowns revealing dimpled bodies, the sparkle of diamonds outshone by rubies and emeralds. I felt out of place among them, an observer, a child in her mother's party dress who'd thought, for just a moment, that she might fit in.

I crossed to an open floor-to-ceiling window, the low sill easily stepped over. My dress caught on the latch and I pulled it free. A thousand golden beads spilled to the paving stones.

Swearing, I turned and inspected the rip. It would be noticeable and reflected in the eyes of the other women. I looked down at the beads scattered at my feet, too small to retrieve, and they sparkled in the light of the party, a tiny galaxy of stars laid aside by a clumsy god.

Stepping into the quiet of the garden, I wished it all away. The party dimmed, became muted, a play on a distant stage, with each step I took across the patio until my feet sank into thick grass. Before me, dark pines rose, concealing wolves and hidden monsters. My shadow ran toward the line of trees, tripping ahead of me. I paused, uneasy, unwilling to turn my back to the trees but wishing to see the house, lit and glowing and shining in the night.

Music moved my muscles, the brassy jazz sliding into a tango, the heat of it touching the base of my spine. I turned.

Every window on the bottom floor shone, curtains open, latches undone so the panes could swing wide in the sultry air. Each held a collection of faces, like walking through an art gallery of paintings that always changed, that continued to shift as I watched.

This crowd twinkled, glistened with makeup and wine, darkened brows lifting and red lips closing around cigarettes. They were alien, gods and goddesses perched on a pinnacle. What had drawn Monroe to me at the Hudsons' party? What did I have that lured him, that tempted, that brought me to this place?

My thoughts conjured him, pulled him into being out of light and noise. He held a single glass of champagne.

"There you are." He crossed the terrace, holding out the glass, cut crystal with a geometric pattern. He pressed it into my hand.

"Thank you." It was cold, as if it had sat in an ice bucket. "The night was so nice, and I wanted a breath of air. Where's yours?" I lifted my champagne.

"Too fizzy for me." Monroe looked around at the trees, darkened like nightmares. "Maybe you'll decide to come in for a dance."

Not a question. I felt a tug, a tingle traveling across my skin. "Of course, I'd love to."

He smiled. "Finish your drink."

I tasted the sparkling wine, savoring the bubbles. Dry and sharp; I would have preferred sweet. He watched me, and I blushed under his gaze, eyes on the house, his want a creature between us.

In the oppressive air it felt as if he already touched me, that his lips had conquered my body, been pressed against intimate places, tongue darting out to taste. My gaze roved over the house, cheeks red with heat.

The top floor sat dark, its black eyes looking out but refusing to let me see in. I wondered what could be upstairs, if tonight I would see a room outfitted in green and gold, feel silk sheets against damp palms.

Movement caught me, stopped me. In the corner window, though dim and seemingly empty, I had seen something. A shadow moved. A figure stepping away. I looked again. Nothing.

I finished my champagne, wanting to be inside. "Shall we?"

He plucked the glass from my hand, bent to lay it on the grass. He took me into his arms, lips against my neck, the hollow behind my ear. He pulled aside the whisper-thin strap of my dress to kiss the spot where it had rested.

"I thought we were going to dance." I said, hands flat against his chest.

"It's the night and your golden dress." Another kiss. "It's too much."

I laughed, turning my head away, pleasure rushing me. My gaze wandered; a pale face watched from that corner room. I stiffened. Monroe took my chin, capturing my attention.

"What's caught your eye?"

I couldn't look away, not with his forefinger and thumb pinning me, the pressure behind his eyes on mine. I waved a hand, vaguely, toward the house. "I thought I saw someone in an upstairs window."

"No one's upstairs."

I turned my head, breaking his grip. The upper windows were empty, no pale face staring out, no movement to suggest that there had been a figure watching.

"One of your guests..."

"There's no one upstairs."

I glanced at him, face impassive, reaching for his hand before unease could change my mind. "Let's have that dance."

He let me pull him toward the house, drawing him away from the odd scene in the grass, leaving those parts of ourselves behind, to fester, to weaken, to die. I refused to bring that part of me. I refused the doubt.

Inside, we danced, the floor crowded, the singer's voice constant. The band played on, eating the night in chunks of time. Monroe danced with me once before I partnered others, men in dark suits, a woman wearing a tuxedo. None wore gold. His eyes found mine, again and again, their darkness flat in the light of the buzzing electric.

"Who did you come with?"

My partner, bluest eyes I've ever seen, spoke.

"I didn't come with anyone."

An eyebrow rose.

"Monroe sent a car for me." I wanted to say it was a Rolls-Royce. I wanted to talk about the color, rich, and the upholstery, velvet. I bit my lip.

"Oh, you're one of his."

I was twirled away, my partner's hand coming back to slip around my waist, tuck me close, welcome me home. I touched my tongue to the roof of my mouth, forming a word that didn't come out. The music ended. A new man appeared, blue eyes moving on.

I asked the question.

"Do you know anything about Monroe?"

There were no answers, nothing beyond a shrug, a slight smile. He was himself, a man with a Rolls-Royce and a large house, a man who appeared to be in possession of the goose who laid the golden egg. I wore the proof.

I looked up after several dances to find Monroe gone, the room crowded but the familiar figure nowhere in it.

I left the floor, refusing a few polite requests for dances, winding past a table laden with drinks to scoop up another glass of champagne. Cold against my hand, I raised the glass to my temple and held it there until my brow cooled. I swayed toward the front of the house, passing the locked front door. I paused, reaching to feel the grain, touch the brass lock.

Spinning, I enjoyed the lightness of champagne flowing through me. A few glanced toward me, away. And, as I twirled, the stairs came into view.

The top sat in darkness, the night come in and sent to bed without supper. I placed my foot on the first rise, feeling the room observing me, refusing to turn, to see.

The next step, and another; I clutched the banister, knuckles going white. I paused at the landing, back straight, quivering with tension. I did look then, a glance out of the corner of my eye. If anyone returned my curiosity, I didn't catch them, and perhaps they were uninterested in the golden girl rising into darkness.

I hesitated on the last stair, considering a line to have been crossed, and then decided. I dove into the beyond, into the places on the other side.

The smell was different here. The open windows downstairs hadn't let enough air in, not enough that it could reach upstairs, to flow along the hall lined with closed doors. No light here. Even the little that followed me up the stairs paused.

I went on alone.

My champagne glass was empty, quickly gone. I stumbled, pausing to set it on the carpet, forgotten as soon as my fingers let go. I stretched my arms wide, unable to touch both walls at once, bouncing between them.

The end came with a crash, sudden in the dark. My own face stared back. I screamed, my hands going to my mouth, stumbling back, tripping to sit abruptly on the carpet. I looked up.

A large mirror reflected black and a distant spark of light at the top of the stairs.

I giggled, falling back, flattening the fashionable knot I'd twisted my long hair into. I hadn't bobbed it but had achieved something almost like one with a few diamond stick pins that pricked me now.

A voice. "Are you alright?" A woman's voice. It stopped my laughter, my heart. Rough, screamed raw, it crept across me, sucking breath from my body. It came lower, in register and location, as if the person were lying flat on the floor, mouth pressed to a crack. "Are you alright?"

I rolled over, facing the voice, reaching out and touching a door. I felt along it, between door and floor, fingers seeking. My heart skipped, stuttered, as I touched someone else's hand.

My fingertips were gripped, the person on the other end skeletal. I could feel the bones, the skin like tissue paper. The voice, the hand, the face I'd seen in the window.

"I am." I whispered, feeling that to speak too loudly would mean the fingers would release, draw back, and I would be left alone in the dark. My laughter from moments before seemed obscene.

I remained connected, taking shallow breathes, the champagne receding. I couldn't hear the party. I couldn't hear the other person. I heard nothing but my own body, the beating and breathing contained by skin.

"You should go."

I shook my head, realized the person couldn't see me. "No one will miss me. The party is so crowded."

"No, leave the house. Go away."

"Come with me."

The fingers disengaged. "The door is locked."

"Wait," I said. I pushed myself up, coming to my knees,

fumbling with the handle of the door. It refused to turn. "Wait." I dared to raise my voice above a whisper, hoping to keep her with me.

I scratched at the door, pushing to my feet, putting my mouth to the seal between door and casing.

"Why is your door locked?"

No answer.

I spoke louder. "Who are you?"

Faint footsteps crossed a room but beneath that, a clink and rattle I couldn't place. "Hush," she said. "Hush or he'll hear you."

"Who?"

"My husband."

I blinked, trying to clear the disquiet that flowed up from the floor, chill anxiety lapping at me. "Your husband owns this house?"

"Yes."

"Monroe?"

I hoped that this time the word, the name, wouldn't conjure the being.

"You need to leave," the woman pleaded. "I saw you, on the lawn. You have to leave. You don't understand."

"Understand what?"

"Unlock the door. Leave the house."

My fingers fumbled with the knob, trying to force rotation, feeling for a latch or lock that I could flip. "I can't unlock your door."

"Not mine. The front door. Go to the front door and unlock it and leave."

"I don't understand."

"You have to leave."

Fear, agitation made me angry, turned my voice sharp. "Stop saying that. I don't understand. Explain."

"There isn't time. No time. You must leave *now*."

"I don't know why you've decided to scare me." I took a step away, leaving the door, putting distance between myself and the voice. "But I think you're being very cruel."

No response.

I retreated another step, going backward, retracing my zigzag path down the hall. The mirror reflected a single dark figure and the light, cautious at the top of the stairs. I wanted to turn, to run for the light, the shelter it offered, but I forced calm into my stride.

The woman spoke. I had to pause, to still my heartbeat, to hold my breath. She repeated herself, again and again, her voice slurring until it became nonsense.

"He'll kill me. He'll kill you."

I ran.

My feet thumped the stairs, down and down, until my body met the front door, rattling it on the hinges. The voices stopped, and I felt them, the watchers, the guests. I couldn't keep my back to them, exposed, thin and white beneath the sheer gold dress. They were like the nightmare trees, observing with malicious intent.

I turned, a hand flying to my face. My cheeks were wet with tears, fingertips tinted black with mascara. Faces stared, the music coming in from the other room, too loud, too cheerful. I scrabbled with the lock, willing it to turn, for the door to open, for the muggy night to embrace me.

"Darling, are you alright?"

I froze. Monroe wove through the crowd, eyes unreadable. The cigar he held smoked, the blue-gray mist trailing him. Then he was at my side, a hand touching my arm, sliding up to my shoulder.

"Where have you been? I looked for you."

His gaze bore into mine, sweat glossing my skin. He saw

my fear, the reflection of it deep in his eyes, a hunter scenting the wounded, the weak. I fumbled with my gown, showed him the rip, the spot where a million beads had jumped free, escaping.

"I tore my dress." I stumbled over my tongue, gone thick, trying to find the words I wanted. "I was looking for the powder room."

His hands touched the rip, but his eyes didn't leave mine. "What a shame."

I inhaled, shook my head. "I'm sorry about the dress. It was an accident. I think I ought to go home now. Too much champagne." I touched my head.

"If you come upstairs, I might have something to mend this." He put pressure on my arm, slight, enough to move me. My feet, they were not mine. They belonged to the woman I'd seen earlier in the mirror at home, a stranger.

The party picked up, continuing, the voices in the hall rising to deaden my internal screams. We moved into an invisible space, ignored by the guests, relegated to an afterthought. My tongue refused to twist, to curve, to form words to capture their attention. I glanced at the door, the white painted wood smeared with mascara. Monroe mounted the first step. I followed, compelled.

I again crossed into the dark, shaking, the hem of my beaded dress dancing, shimmying. I gulped air, chest tightening, hot and cold crawling over me.

"I see you've already been here." He scooped up the glass I'd forgotten, holding it up in a mock toast. "To us. 'Till death." He threw it shattering into the wall, sending shivers over my skin. A smile as he reached for me, touched me.

I jumped, pausing, opening my mouth to deny.

"The gold fit you well. Better than some."

I tried to tug my arm free. His hold tightened, biting. "I think it's time for me to go home."

Monroe changed his grip, tucking me against him. His heart beat beside mine, through bone and blood, skin and fabric. He led me to the end of the hall. The mirror reflected two dark figures. Monroe jingled keys free from his pocket, the slide of metal against metal singing in my ears. The lock sprang open. I heard him search for the switch, the click of it.

Light filled the space and I knew exactly how it would look from outside, standing on the dark lawn and looking up; a single golden window on the second floor.

The interior shone red, metal clinking, a pair of flat eyes huge and dark. I couldn't see her, not all at once, not with my stuttering brain and tears swimming across my vision.

Monroe smiled, covering a distance there would never be between us again. "'Till death do us part," he said, and took a step toward her.

3

TRAVEL PERMIT

Roughly 40 Million Years Ago

"I'm sorry," she said into his chest.

"It's okay." He smoothed her hair. "It upset me too."

She looked up, pushing herself away a little, meeting his gaze. He smiled, gentle and kind, understanding, reached up to brush his fingers across her cheek. She returned the smile. He bent his head, mouth hovering. "Okay?" he breathed.

"Okay," she said.

They kissed on a black sand beach, a lava flow half a mile away sending up plumes of steam as it sank into the Pacific. His hands tangled in her hair, tears on her cheeks not yet dry. They stood at the birth of an island, at the edge of a beginning.

1793

The blade sang as it descended, a high note cutting

across the rumbling murmur of the crowd. Vast, a frothing foaming body of faces, eager and upturned to feel the splatter and catch the final exhalation. Those nearest pressed forward, swiping handkerchiefs through the blood, waving reddened flags above their heads.

Darcy fought to catch her breath, to tamp down rising nausea. Sweat glossed her face, rolled down her back. She was pushed and stumbled, catching herself on the person in front of her. The crowd surged, ravenous for a piece of the dead queen. Her head rose, hoisted on a pike. Darcy put her hand to her mouth.

"Want to go?"

Evan's voice, his hand on her arm, brought her back. The crowd shifted again, trapping the pair in the slipstream. She half turned to him, tears mixing with horror, wondering why she'd ever added this one to the list. She found his face, his steady eyes.

The scene melted, the world focusing to his gaze, the feel of his hands on her shoulders, the warmth of him in front of her. The metallic scent lingered, even so far from the machine, the smell of unwashed bodies and rabid fury. Darcy squeezed her eyes shut, wishing it away.

1906

Her favorite president.

Theodore Roosevelt.

Darcy smiled as he spoke, at his larger-than-life gestures. As large as history. His glasses reflected Congress. The room reverberated with occupants murmuring behind hands. She stood in his periphery, smiling because he was everything she'd ever read. He fought for the creation of a National Parks system, stressing the importance, mustache bristling, arm a piston going up and down.

"Why do you like him?" Evan whispered against her ear.

She shrugged, "Always have."

"Got a thing for blustery old white men?"

She covered her mouth with a hand, smiling into her palm. This moment was history, a marker placed in time on a roadmap unchanged by travelers. She'd stapled a list of dates to the Travel Permit; long and handwritten, it continued on the back and slanted at an angle on the unlined paper. This date had been starred, folded page bulging in her back pocket. The red approval stamp sat at the bottom of her purse.

"What's next?"

She pulled the pages free, borrowed a pen from a desk nearby. "The Terror."

His face blanched. "Why?"

"I had someone come in this morning for a permit and the date got stuck in my head." He reached for her hand, the spark of him electric. "If you're sure."

"We're going everywhen, remember?"

She watched their joined hands instead of the blurring figure, his words fading into the white noise of a crowd.

1869

"Hold on!" He reached out, stopped her from toppling over the edge.

Darcy looked around, unsure of where they'd landed, dust rolling into a red and orange landscape. Overhead a bright clear sky spread from horizon to horizon. They stood on the lip of a canyon, sweating in the heat of a lowering sun.

"I thought we were going to see Powell?"

"There!" Evan pointed to where the Colorado River, snaking at the bottom of the canyon, came into view. Down the middle, a large boat filled with men rowed, tiny at this distance.

John Wesley Powell.

"I'm related to him somehow," Darcy said. "That's what my mom told me. I don't know how. I did a report once in school, all about how he mapped the river."

"Maybe that's where you got your spirit of adventure?"

Darcy let out a laugh. "Took long enough for it to show up."

1510

"Do you think he knows?"

Darcy lifted a brow, almost shrugged. "It's so good. I don't know how he couldn't."

"But do we really see that far? It's years, it's centuries. Lifetimes."

The artist lifted a brush. Russet color swept down, becoming a fold of fabric. The cream and milk flesh of the child glowed, the moon face of the Madonna sweet.

Titian grumbled as he worked.

1969

Darcy put her fingers in her ears, but the music came through, vibrating up from the floor and into the soles of her feet. The arena below her, around her, rolled with collected smoke and flashed with upheld lighters; an unknown galaxy shimmering. On the stage the singer strutted, bellowing his lines, the voices of the crowd a delayed echo.

The Stones.

Evan sang. She glanced at him, taking pieces of his face with her, turning them over in her mind, not wanting to be caught staring. His sandy hair and blue eyes, the dimple in his right cheek. Even so close she couldn't distinguish his voice from the rest, but heat and an agony of butterflies thrilled through her every time his arm brushed hers.

———

2084

"If you could visit your parents, wouldn't you?"

"Mine aren't dead. I'm adopted."

He looked at her, "You're lucky to have them."

Darcy nodded. "Wrinkled carrots and all."

They stood in silence then, watching the couple through the lit window. The world was dark around them, spangled and singing with the voices of a thousand night insects. In the square a young couple moved about a galley kitchen, the woman armed with a wooden spoon and the man struggling to open a bottle of wine. Pots steamed on the stovetop. A radio perched on the counter. Darcy told herself she could hear the music.

"They look happy."

———

Friday

"Mr. Organdy's permit application is for the Terror. Marie Antoinette's execution."

Ms. Pin opened a large red leather book on her desk, flipping through thin whispering pages. She licked a finger, touched it to the page. "Date?"

"October 16, 1793."

"And he's wanting to take two minors?"

"A history lesson."

"It's rated R. What're their ages?"

"Nine and eleven."

"His kids?"

Darcy nodded, the permit application in her hand blue with ink pen and smudged with white-out. Her feet ached, dull and constant, the big toes pinched by shoes that had looked comfortable but had lied. She shifted, leaned against the open door to the office.

"Too young."

"He says they're studying it in school and he'd like them to see it for themselves."

"Reading about it and seeing it are two very different things. At fifteen they can go with a parent. Until then, no."

The book slammed shut. Ms. Pin went back to her computer. Her large glasses reflected spreadsheets and numbers, rows and rows bullied into order. Darcy hesitated, seeing the father's face, his pout as she checked the application his look when she'd said she'd check with the boss.

"What?" Ms. Pin didn't look up.

"He's very determined." Darcy folded the corner of the paper over, creasing it with a nail. "He says it's important for their class project."

Ms. Pin stood, shaking her head, smoothing down the

wool skirt as she came out from behind the desk. She took the permit application from Darcy as she passed, marching to the service counter where Mr. Organdy waited. If her shoes were too tight, it wasn't apparent, the sensible flats connected to thin calves encased in hunter green tights. Ms. Pin, sharp as her name, looked like a tall bird, raised high on skinny legs and crowned with flyaway hair she insisted on coloring an unnatural shade of red. Darcy touched her own hair, a dark outgrown bob on the way to being shoulder length, and followed with a twist of unease.

The man glowered at the pair, one tall and one plump, and looked as if he thought he could stare them into submission. Ms. Pin raised an eyebrow, sliding the permit application across the counter.

"Winnie, would you please approve this thing, so I can get back to work? I'm on my lunch hour here, trying to get the trip settled for the kids." Implication lurked in his voice. Darcy had been less than helpful intentionally.

Ms. Pin smiled, her eyes cold. "Mr. Organdy, I'm afraid we can't approve your permit. The children listed are underage for that historical event."

"They're studying it in school. There's no reason they shouldn't see it." He pinned the permit with a forefinger, slid it back.

"I'm afraid those are the rules. The material they would witness is not suitable for minors. Our new director announced the changes. Perhaps you'd like to make an appointment with him?"

Mr. Organdy looked from Ms. Pin to Darcy, with his tailored gray suit the color of his eyes and hair, a monochrome man with a reddening face. Ms. Pin picked up the phone, finger hovering over the button for the direct line upstairs. "Shall I call his personal assistant and let him know you're on your way?"

He scowled, the permit crumpled in one hand and tossed at the recycling basket behind Darcy. She flinched, biting the inside of her cheek. Mr. Organdy didn't notice, already out the door and on his way to the parking lot. Ms. Pin set the phone down and turned to Darcy. "Dig out that permit and send it upstairs with a note. If he takes his kids through a back door, we want to make sure we're covered."

"Of course." Darcy rummaged, pulling it out and smoothing it on the corner of her desk behind the counter.

Ms. Pin retreated to her office with the crooked name-plate on the door. The carpet between her office and the service counter had been worn down, a ragged trail of back and forth. Darcy wrote a quick explanation on the crumpled paper and dropped it in the outbox.

A stack of travel permits sat waiting to be approved, several of the blue-inked documents greasy with food stains. Last month's color had been luminescent pink, and the printers had used an ink that came off on the skin, leaving Darcy with magenta fingers. This month's color, a pale blue, appeared to be more permanent but harder to read. The light overhead flickered, buzzing. She reached for her approved stamp, bright red, and brought it thumping down in the square approval box at the bottom. Her initials were added, and she set it aside to be mailed back at the end of the day.

Time travel, once an ultimate luxury, had become an everyday thing overseen by a small branch of the government from two rooms on separate floors. The location of the offices was not intentional. The director of Time Travel Permits had been moved from an office adjacent to Ms. Pin's to a room upstairs, because he'd complained about the lack of a private restroom. His new office, his desk and file cabinet on one wall with his personal assistant's desk on the other, was a pass-through from a common eating area and the large upstairs men's restroom.

Darcy had never complained about buying her own office supplies. She worried that they might take the money for new paperclips from her bimonthly.

Ms. Pin managed the math involved with the permits, Darcy approved or denied, Mr. Henry, the director, handled public relations and other branches of the government, and his assistant, Josephine, niece of someone important getting a degree in Ridged History, did her homework in the shared office. She traveled a lot for research, but the director had yet to approve her going anywhen really dangerous.

Darcy had celebrated her fourth anniversary yesterday. Not once had she ever approved her own Travel Permit.

She stamped and initialed her way through the stack, squinting at handwriting and occasionally looking up dates for events or looking up events for seemingly random dates. No one ever managed to fill in the entire form, despite the bold print at the top asking that it be completed. If people had followed the bold print she wouldn't have a job.

At lunch she wandered upstairs to the break room and cut herself a piece of cake. It had read *Congratulations, Darcy! Four More Years!* Ms. Pin's doing, her kindness. Now only her name remained in purple icing on white. The middle had been excavated, everyone who'd wandered away with a piece firmly in the adult world wanting to avoid the diabetic coma the corner pieces with extra icing entailed.

She took the stairs, armed with a plastic fork and looking forward to the rest of the afternoon, the downhill slide. From now until five, she had permits and cake, tea at four.

The afternoon eased by. At a quarter to five, someone coughed.

She looked at the clock on the corner of her computer screen, stomach sinking. In her experience anyone who came at the end of the day usually had issues with a permit that would require her to remain in the building past five.

The cough, however, had been apologetic, as if the owner knew that his issue might encroach on her valuable time. Darcy looked up, smiling because she was the kind of woman who greeted everyone with a smile even while resenting them for keeping her late.

The man returned her smile. She focused on his chipped front tooth. It was the only imperfection.

"Hi."

"Hello," she said.

"I have some questions about a permit."

She pushed back her chair. "Do you have it with you?"

"No."

"Okay." She stood, crossing to the shelf behind her to take a blue permit from the correctly marked slot. She placed it on the counter, eyes on the form. "Fill this out. If everything's good I'll approve it before you leave. You'll have to take it to the ticket agency to collect the actual passes. But you'll need to keep it with you at all times in case of an emergency."

"What happens if I have an emergency?"

"Well, when you pick up your passes, they'll have a one-time emergency signal for you to activate. Help will arrive, and your Permit will be verified."

"So, I could be," he waved a hand, "attacked by dinosaurs, burning at the stake, or about to be killed by an oncoming train, and they'll want to see my permit first?"

Darcy didn't answer. He smiled. She didn't. He coughed.

"So, permit. Yeah. Name."

He mumbled as he filled it out at the counter. Darcy straightened the stacks of blank permits in the rack behind her desk, shuffling and reshuffling. Her eyes rolled to the clock on the wall behind the man. It was five minutes fast, and office hours were quickly coming to a close.

Dinner. What would she have for dinner? Leftovers. Or she could stop at the market and pick up something fresh. But then she'd have to cook. Takeout. She could order it on the way home. Pick it up. Cat food, she needed cat food. Her neighbor was cruising the Bahamas with pirates. She'd promised to feed the cat. It ate special food, refrigerated, had to be purchased fresh every few days. Spoiled rotten cat.

"So," the man said, "have you ever gone?"

Maybe the cat would eat leftovers. What did she have? Pot roast, wrinkled carrots from dinner at her parents' house.

"I'm sorry?"

"You travel?" He tapped the permit with the pen.

Darcy shook her head, reaching for the paper. "Finished?"

"I'm Evan."

She met his gaze, "What?"

He tapped his chest with the pen, "Evan."

She glanced at the name section at the top of the form, *Evan Richards the Seventeenth*. "Seventeenth?"

"It's a name with a lot of history."

She nodded, looking over the rest, scanning. Name, address, employer, insurance information, next of kin. She went back to employer, the address for the location was this building, her building. The Office of Mandatory Moral Improvement or MMI for short.

"You work upstairs?"

"Walk past here most days, Darcy."

She stopped, met his eyes. He tapped the nameplate that sat to the side of the counter, *Darcy Matheson* in Helvetica. She smiled tightly, gaze dropping.

"I'm really having to work hard here."

"You didn't fill out the where or when."

They spoke at the same time, their voices mixing, melding. He laughed.

"Where?" He leaned forward, and she held the page out, pointing. "Oh yeah, I left that for you to fill in."

She opened her mouth. Shut it. Settled on, "Excuse me?"

"When do you want to go?"

She shook her head. "We'll be closing in less than five minutes. If you want a permit for the weekend you really need to fill this out."

He reached, tapping the page. "It's for two."

"I assume you have a friend."

He smiled a perfect smile, a charming smile, a devil-may-care, melt-your-bones kind of smile. "Go with me."

"I have to feed my cat."

He laughed. "Come on, you've never gone. Why not go with a big strapping guy who can protect you from all the crazies history has to offer?"

"That's what emergency signals are for."

He nodded, "True. But will emergency signals hold your purse? I'll totally hold your purse."

Darcy laughed, a bark of amusement that surprised her, that surprised him. His grin broadened.

"Come with me."

She shook her head. "Thanks for the offer, but no."

He hesitated, searching her face. "Will you approve it without the dates filled in?"

"Can't do that."

"Okay." He took it, scribbled in a date and handed it back.

Darcy looked at the date, creasing her brow. She turned to go into Ms. Pin's office, to search the giant red leather book.

"It's not going to be in there."

She turned back to him. "When is this? What's there?"

"The date my dad told my mom he loved her for the first time."

Darcy looked at him for a long moment. She could feel it sliding by in the ticking of the clock. He held her gaze and she wondered why he'd picked that date, what he'd hoped he might convey. She picked up the red approval stamp, the thump of it hitting the page closing her eyes. She initialed it.

"So I guess it's too late to add any other destinations?" he asked.

"You can always add dates, just staple a separate sheet to this one. But they'll still have to be approved. I'll just initial them now if you've got them ready."

He shook his head. "I was just wondering. For next time, you know?"

She nodded. "Sure."

He knocked the counter with his knuckles, smiled at her. "Thanks so much for your help. And you know, if you change your mind, I'll be walking really slowly to my car." He waved the permit at her.

"Thanks, I appreciate the offer, but I really do have a cat to feed."

He smiled, thin and tight and left. Darcy sat, staring at her screen. 5:08 PM.

Ms. Pin called from her office. "Don't worry about locking up tonight, Darcy. I'm going to be working late. You can head home whenever you're ready."

Home. Leftovers. Spoiled cat. Darcy pressed the start button on the computer; it gave a disgruntled beep before shutting down. The approval stamp lay on the red ink pad. She grabbed it, snatching up her bag and running for the door, uncomfortable shoes ignored.

She caught him in the parking lot.

4

ISAAC

He carried a vintage makeup case, powder blue with a pale satin lining. The mirror inside cracked, throwing back the world, showing his face broken and pieced together in a way that made him more beautiful. He stood a few inches taller than me, a few years older. At seven with black hair and darker eyes, my mother claimed I'd be a girl all the boys noticed when the time came. But only Isaac saw me.

While I slept he took the contents of the case and placed them on my front step: spotted eggshells, tight green pine cones, a glossy black beetle with curled up legs, an opalescent piece of shed snakeskin.

My parents, if they noticed, didn't say anything. I missed their exchanged smiles above my head; smiles like words, thinking they saw something I could not.

And when he knocked on the door and my mother called my name, I ran down the stairs in cutoff shorts and scabbed knees.

"Isaac's here," she said, stepping back until I saw him framed by the screen door.

"I have something to show you."

I turned to my mother, "Can I go?" An echo of a children's game, *Mother May I?*

"Be back for dinner."

Out of sight of my duplex he takes my hand. "Come with me."

My heart beats in my palm, the heat of his skin on mine making me sweat and wonder what might happen if he intertwined his fingers with mine. But he holds my hand like my mother does, like my father; he takes my hand to pull me along.

We go down alleys, looking at the backs of houses until we reach a hill with a ragged path. The earth is dry, dusty and thirsty. It absorbs my sweat, the moisture disappearing as soon as it appears on my skin.

I don't ask him where we're going. We don't speak. I see what he wanted to show me.

A gray rag of fur, skeletal, red ants crawling all over it. A rabbit, dead of drought, the earth sucking it dry. The summer had been filled with these delicate decaying bodies, bleaching under a too close sun.

I squat, watching the ants move over the fur in lines, geometric patterns of nature. Isaac crouches beside me, the blue makeup case between us. Reaching out, no hesitation or shaking fingers, he places his hands on the dead thing.

Ants swirl up his arms, biting, red spots swelling. He doesn't speak, doesn't look at me. I taste panic, reach out to brush them from his skin, but he shakes his head. Beneath his hands the carcass plumps, swells, a back leg twitches. The dead eye blinks. An exhale sends a tiny puff of dust rushing away from the rabbit.

Beneath Isaac's hands it rolls, coming to its feet, shaking ants away. Ears twitch, one way and another, liquid eyes rolling toward us. I can see the too quick beat of its heart, breath that comes and goes so fast with fear.

It bolts. For a moment Isaac's hands remain cupped around a rabbit-shaped hole. It's gone, disappeared into olive brush and eucalyptus trees, leaving hungry ants.

I stand, up on the tips of toes, to see if I can spot it going down the hill. And there at a distance, growing finer and smaller, the gray rabbit is running.

Beside me, Isaac laughs.

5

MISSING

HE GUTTED THE ELK, muscles in his neck and back jumping, skin slick with a sheen of sweat. I watched the muddy red earth beneath his feet, not the slip-and-slide of purple-red organs as they fell to the ground. The clearing hummed with the act, his lack of hesitation.

The cavity left behind pulled at my eye.

Meredith, my pale older cousin on Mother's side, sharp-featured with a wide mouth. She invited kisses and confidences and I watched as she spoke; color fading, going from rosy to white. The family talked as if she weren't in the room, as if her senses had failed and not her body. She heard them, looking out of plum dark eyes, her fingers knotted, finer than handmade lace.

Meredith, dying, but loved.

I think the poets got it wrong, this idea of love. Matthew thought it would be enough, that it would be food and air, water and life. Even at thirteen I knew it couldn't be all. I watched them hook up tubes and pump liquids through her like a machine, Mother standing next to my aunt, their hands clasped. Matthew always at her side, there, unshaven, reeking of hand sanitizer. I think toward the end he stopped showering. Even the few minutes getting clean took away from her.

I wore thick glasses and acne dotted my skin. *Wash your face, you'll grow out of it.* But the growing wasn't happening soon enough, and when I saw the way Matthew looked at Meredith it made something inside me ache. I didn't want him, not exactly, but I wanted a man to see me that way. To recognize the girl beneath the spots and lack of enthusiasm for all things school-related. I wanted to be an adult.

Her death was witnessed. That word, like the hard chopping motion of a cleaver coming down on a cutting board. *This far and no more,* it seemed to say. A huddle of us in the room, the bed lit from above with pain medication easing the way, the hushed voices and tears.

I was a part and not a part of it, relegated to the back due to age. But from where I stood I could see Matthew, and I think I was the only one watching him. The monitors had been turned off. We didn't need them to see her lungs fail and a slackness spread across a body that had been taut with pain. Matthew spoke, whispering her name, for the first time in a week.

Meredith.

Mother wailed, my aunt crumpling to the bed, and the rest of the family closed in, a blossom pulling tight. In all of that, Matthew stood and retreated, walking by me without a glance, as if I weren't there, leaning against the wall with a perfect teenage slouch.

He looked robbed, as if something had been stolen, outrage and anger, sorrow and need on his face. He burned, cheeks flushed and mouth tight. He looked as if he'd rip down the sky, split the skin of the earth, pull Meredith whole from the remains.

I followed, half hoping he'd see me and turn, half hoping he'd hear me and say my name. A crush, like when I was eight and convinced that the world would end if the ten-year-old up the street didn't hold my hand. But less than that because I realized it was fantasy, and not the kind I would want to come true, just a dream for my future.

I followed because with Meredith gone I wasn't sure what else could keep him here. He'd been a regular face at family events, with kind eyes, a bottle of wine in hand. Once there had been a gift of Necco Wafers, something no one else seemed to like but me, something I wouldn't have to share. But whenever we pressed him for information about his family, brothers or sisters, grandparents and uncles, the answer was *none*. He came from a past with no photos or stories, with no trail of breadcrumbs to follow back. He was alone except for us.

So I followed Matthew into the woods because he was alone, except for me.

Mother calls me Sylvie, like Sylvia Plath who stuck her head in an oven. It's a terrible thing to name a child. Meredith said it could have been much worse, I could have been Ophelia, but I think drowning might be better than gassing. Though a name not associated with death would have been preferred. But no, I am Sylvie, with zits and glasses, and years of verbal torture ahead.

I am Sylvie who walked with Matthew into the woods and watched him kill an elk.

I chased him from the hospital, into the parking lot where his car sat. He pulled a pistol from the glove box, big and black, sucking the world to a point. I thought he'd shoot himself, so I screamed his name, ran to him. He looked down at me with dark eyes, his face a blank wash. He was like those dry creeks running though the desert, no water but you can see where it had been, where it took sand and rock away, leaving an empty stretch of land.

"Where are you going?"

Without speaking he extended a hand. I took it, his fingers cold around mine. In the other he kept the gun and we turned as one to the trees at the edge of the parking lot.

I think all woods connect. I think there is a spot where you walk between two trunks and are someplace else. There will always be a moment when you look back the way you've come and realize it looks nothing like it did when you walked in. Matthew led me between two trees and the world around us shifted, just slightly, just enough.

He squeezed my hand, two counts of gentle pressure,

and then we walked. Leaves crunched beneath our feet, a breeze rustling after. It took me a moment to see the animal. He was so large my brain hadn't registered him as my eye slid over the dark shape. Then I saw the antlers and my brain said *elk* but larger than any I had ever seen.

The animal approached, head high, antlers brushing low-hanging branches. I took a step back, remembering every video I'd seen of wild animals attacking people on the internet. The elk stretched its neck, nostrils flared. Its breath fogged, touching me.

I didn't see the pistol raised, didn't see him aim. But I jumped at the shot, vibration traveling from him up our joined hands and into my tightening jaw. It rang, throbbing through the trees, the solid trunks throwing back the noise. My ears hummed with the sound, my free hand coming up to try to keep the high whine out.

The elk buckled at the knees. At first I didn't think it had been hit; I couldn't see a wound. But then a wet streak of blood appeared, and I saw a hole in the animal's forehead. Matthew started forward, still grasping my hand, but I pulled back, held back. He released me and went on, leaving me clutching empty air, dropping the pistol and taking a folding knife from his jeans. I watched him strip down to boxers, kicking off his shoes.

I had to look away when he began to cut.

A clean shot, a bullet too small to stop an animal so big, and yet it parted flesh. Matthew stood bloody to the shoulders, torso smeared, boxers clinging. He didn't speak, and I wondered if his tongue had fused to the roof of his mouth. I wanted him to say something, anything, and I would think it normal, I would assume he was crazed with grief and nothing else.

He lifted the elk hide, the head drooping, skin moving in unnatural ways; the legs flopping, dragging, and seemingly unattached. But he wrapped it around himself, antlers sitting atop his head, the face of the elk falling to cover his own. A flash of white, his hand pulling the parted skin together, and then there was not a man but a deformed animal standing in the woods. He began to walk.

Stumbling after I stepped in the offal left behind, the warmth of it soaking into my jeans, I cried out, the smell terrible, like something dead. *It is dead*. The elk that was not, eyes blinking, shaking its head as if its ears buzzed. The skin had mended, knitting together. Odd lumps moved beneath the flesh, as if something did not quite fit, but as I watched the beast straightened, standing tall on hind legs.

The human face was gone.

I extended a hand. The beast dropped to all four limbs, the earth shivering. The urge to run turned my skin to ice and fire, my legs trembling, teeth chattering. It advanced, legs stiff, the flesh across its shoulders rolling. A round hairless spot marked where a bullet might have entered the skull.

A snuff of warm breath touched my fingers; the scent of a wild animal that is familiar but not engulfed me, like a barnyard full of cows and something like a deer. I was dwarfed and exposed, looking into familiar brown eyes.

I left the wood carrying the gun, blood on the bottoms of my sneakers, leaving rebirth behind so that I could face the death of Meredith. They searched for him, my family and the police. They found his clothes, found the offal, found blood and tracks that led away, deeper into the wood.

Never Matthew.

6

DEEP WATER

I STRIP to the murmuring approval of the sea.

Fabric peels away to reveal white flesh pebbled with cold, nipples hard. The wind takes the clothes, rushing them, rolling, down the stone beach. I hunch my shoulders, ignore the loss.

The first touch is welcome, a homecoming, and water crawls up my shins. It rises, licking, tasting old scars and scabbed knees as I walk forward; a laugh lurking at the bottom of my gut ripples, bubbling, breaking. I open my arms, welcoming the curling cling of the waves.

He screams.

Another step and slick seaweed is between my toes, my name blending with the grumble of the sea. He's frantic, the edge of his voice rasping my ears, turning them red. I want to dive and swim out to the horizon, reach that edge and slip over, fall out of the known world.

A bite halts me, abrupt as breaking bone, fire spreading from my shoulder blade. I glance back to see him on the beach, armed with a deep-sea fishing rod. We are connected by filament fine as spider silk, invisible as it leaves his hand, invisible until it touches me. I rub salt water from my eyes, heat sweeping from the hook in my shoulder. The tide tugs at my body, pushing at my thighs, my hips.

"You aren't the right shape, Sophie!"

The sun is high and bright in a cloudless sky. He's come home early. I thought he'd be out on the boat, gone away only to come back. But he's caught me. Again.

"If you keep going you'll only get torn up."

He won't let go of the rod, of me. He'd haul me back naked, bloody, shaking with cold.

I clutch the line, dragging him into the crashing waves. My shoulder rips, warm blood running down my back, clouding the water. Tossing the rod away, he stumbles, then comes to me, the waves willing us together.

He pulls the barb free, hands darting over my skin. The water rises, licking between my legs, kissing my hips, my lower stomach, cooling flesh heated with contact. His clothes drink the sea, beneath them a hot furnace he presses against me. Hip to hip, forcing submission, his mouth covers mine, demanding I forget, requesting I stay.

I stay.

He hurries me toward the stone beach, out of the calling sea, to a land filled with pebbles worn flat and rubbed raw. I quiver in a gust of wind, damp hair slapping against my back. The waves roll after me, then away, sucking at earth with each retreat.

"Where're your clothes?"

I shake my head.

John's vivid orange coat lies wadded past the water line, a deformed crab. He stands me still, a hand on my elbow as if I might dart away. He throws it around me, fastening the buttons with shaking fingers. It comes down to my knees, shivering in time with trembling muscles.

John talks, words tumbling around me. I listen, not to their sense, but to the tone, the pattern he weaves.

"Don't you know I love you?"

The question lingers, waiting for an answer. I nod, allowing him to lead me through scrubby brush on bare feet to his waiting truck that smells like fish, old rope, salt, sweat. It smells like the sea. I pause at the door, turning toward the ocean. The rough hush whisper of water creeping up the beach, inspecting the stones I'd stepped across, crawling, crying after me.

I sit on stained fabric. He leans in to fasten the belt, the key on a chain around his neck swinging free. He's close, eyes meeting mine in the tight space. They're green like knee-deep moss. He presses another kiss on me, tasting of salt and air exhaled by dolphins and whales, tinted with seaweed and bubbly kelp. Earth and sea, land and water, he is both in his kiss. I lick my lips as he rounds the truck and slides in beside me.

The engine turns, catches, rumbles. The vibration thrums, and I clutch the seat. A crust of salt dries on my skin, my hair.

"The front door was open, stove on." He watches the road, shifting and gassing the truck. "You left it all behind on a whim."

He doesn't sound angry. He can't understand that playing housewife wouldn't appeal to something wild.

I look through glass, smelling his forgotten lunch and the reek of waterlogged rope in the back seat. The sea has gone from my window, vanished in a curve of pavement. I wait, anticipating where it'll reappear; the trees part, exposing a distant expanse of hard blue.

He is a bird, an eagle, that fell in love with a fish and snatched her from the sea.

When the truck stops I look at the weatherworn cabin perched at the top of a cliff. The wood pile tilts against the east wall, high as the eves; an outhouse at a distance, and a spring even farther away. Here we're on the back side of summer, a short fall approaching and then the deep black days of an Alaskan winter.

At the cliff edge I can look out, see the backs of seagulls, see where sky touches water and stars disappear. I wonder, sometimes, if he first saw me here. My seal face peering above the waves, inspecting the shore.

I clutch his coat tight, picking my way up the gravel path and inside. So faint it breaks my heart the cabin smells of the sea.

A pot of water boils on the stove, beside forgotten fish stew from that morning. I ignore the locked closet door, glance at the metal tub set before the unlit fire.

Fingers pluck at the shoulders of the coat. I turn, so he can fumble with the buttons. He peels the fabric away, lets it pool at my feet.

"I'll get a bath ready."

A match is struck, hot water transferred and cold added until it will turn my skin delicate pink. He beckons, and I take his hand, stepping over the rim of the tub, crouching to feel warmth against private flesh.

I exhale, rubbing my hands over my face. Almond soap is smoothed over me, John's mouth thin and hands gentle. I shut my eyes when he dumps a bucket over me, rinsing my hair. He presses his face against my back. I sit, rigid, listening to him breathe.

"I can't let you go." He whispers, a promise, a prayer, a threat, but there's sorrow beneath the current. His body, my body, it is our body, even with the tin bath separating us.

Then he stands. I follow, water sloshing, accepting the

robe he holds. I sit before the fire, combing the memory of sea salt kisses from my hair. He rubs ointment on my hook bite, covering it with a bandage. His hands linger, one on my shoulder, the other following the curve of my spine. With a groan he stands, leaving cool air.

The generator coughs, electric light joins firelight, and then the mellow chords of the record player reach out.

"Dance with me, Sophie."

With one hand at the back of his neck, the other held against his heart, we sway; his cheek, whiskery abrasive, smoothes over mine. I play with his hair, soft curling strands, and he sighs.

Outside, north of the Arctic Circle and trapped by meaningless time, the sun sulks against the horizon. The needle slips off the record, hissing white noise. I move away toward the kitchen, reach for two glasses and the whiskey from the top cabinet.

John stands where I left him, profile an old coin, the hook of his nose giving him a sinister edge. Until he looks at me, until he smiles, and then sweet melting softness shows through; an ordinary face becoming extraordinary, rare. I put the tumblers in his hands, splashing generous amounts into each. Recovering mine, I throw it back, cough. He drinks his own, bending to refill. We do this until the room becomes a sucking whirlpool.

"I watched you on the rocks, naked, soaking up sun for hours. Like the stories. I almost didn't believe it until I touched your fur." John speaks, imparting a tale, a slice of tall fiction. "I never thought you'd leave."

He's never shared, and it takes time, his eyes on the floor. I reach out to touch the key around his neck. He tracks the movement, and I lift it over his head. I ask a wordless question. John gives a whiskey shrug.

The key fits, finding a mate in the hollow lock. It clicks as it turns; the open door reveals rifles, a safe with a turn dial eye. A seal skin sits folded on the top shelf. I cry into the warmth, rubbing my cheeks against silken fur.

John takes a swaying step, touches me. He plucks at the robe until I stand exposed. He tugs his clothes off, stumbling, knocking over the empty bottle. I consume his nakedness, roving over muscles gained from working fishing lines and crab pots, the scars and dark hair matting his chest, the nest of his genitals.

He takes the fur, shakes it out; the hollow eyes catch light, flash yellow. It settles around me, and I run a hand over the seal face, my face. Catching my hand, pressing a kiss into the palm, he pulls me to the door. The Alaskan never night is a witness as we run down the steps, through the yard, pausing at the cliff edge.

I smile with hunter's teeth and squeeze his hand. I never considered jumping from here. But with my sleek skin, I'd make it. I take my hand from his, but he reclaims it.

We leap, with no birds to witness our fall. My skin clings, becoming me. Then the crashing cold, a shock, forcing breath from my body, but I surface, swimming. John looks surprised, face to the cliff we have dropped from like a pair of diving puffins.

Then he turns. He sees me. *Me.*

I have no hand to extend, no fingers to entwine, no arms in the way he knows them. But he holds on as we both suck in air, dive.

I take him home.

7

GIRL WITH THE GLASSES

SARA COVERT LIVED at the end of the road, down far enough that half the time I forgot she was there. I think everyone else did too; her blonde head shone like a beacon as she walked down the middle of the gravel road, surprising everyone at the bus stop as they recalled her forgotten face.

Blonde, the kind that goes white with summer sun, and thick glasses that were a peachy pink plastic. Like a small bird she'd come among us, feathers ruffled up, eyes down and searching for the next foothold on our strange territory. I started watching her at school, the way she walked the halls with classroom folders pressed to her flat chest, the sidestepping way she avoided brushing against anyone at the last moment.

It was Christmas break before I said anything, out in the woods, the trees holding up a snowy sky. My feet were frozen almost solid, the kind of cold that you stop feeling, the kind that burns when your momma puts your feet in a tub of hot water. I held a branch covered in ice, coated like sugar and spendthrift stars, something I'd hacked free and declared to be a magic wand. I was practicing to be the Ice Queen, and I think I was pretty good at it.

"I like your wand."

The voice, small and high, flitting from behind trees and out from the low sky, caught me, held me still in a grip that sent my heart stuttering. Then she stepped into my line of sight, coming from behind two trees that didn't seem wide enough to hide the blue-jacketed body. A yellow bobble hat mocked her blonde hair, and her eyes shimmered at me, the smile tentative.

"Thanks," I said, giving it a royal swish.

I'm not sure if we discussed it first—I don't think you need to when you're under ten and the world is made of up friends. We played, taking turns with the iced wand, the sun slinking down, wallowing into violet dark.

"Angie!"

My momma's voice from a distance, calling like a crow, the name coming out in two long syllables. It came again, a strange nighttime creature hunting only for me.

"Gotta go!" I said, thrusting the branch into her hand. "You can keep it!"

I stumbled home, half running, my momma bawling out the back door until she saw me coming out of the trees into the yard. She took one look at my face and started in. "What have I told you about staying out so long in the cold? Get inside and get those things off. You're having a hot bath and a hot drink, and then if your homework isn't done you can finish that. Jesus girl, your face looks half frozen."

A mumbled *yes mamma* was all it took because it was never a question of her being wrong.

A few days later school started, and I saw the girl in the glasses at the bus stop. I watched the tiny figure come down the road, trudging along. I waved my arm until it about fell off, feeling like an idiot because I couldn't remember her name. But when she finally looked up and saw me, it was worth it to see the smile on her face.

Then I remembered. "Hey, Sara!"

For the rest of the year we stood together at the bus stop, mostly in silence, sometimes talking quietly about the things we spotted in the woods.

"I saw a wren today."

"I saw a doe."

"I saw a fat silver fish in the creek."

"I saw a rabbit."

"I saw a hawk."

"I saw a bird with a yellow belly."

"I saw a snake."

I saw, I saw, I saw, the game went on. She must have spent the night at my house a hundred times before I was even invited to step through her front door. My momma had short quick conversations on the phone, never quite believing that Sara had delivered nothing but the whole truth when she said, "Yes ma'am, my momma said it was okay to spend the night on a school night."

Sometimes, when it was just me in the house, I'd hear my parents talking in the kitchen.

"It's like she's being raised by wolves. I get one-word responses to questions and she only calls once a month, if even that, to make sure Sara made it to school or home on the nights she's with us. Any note I send along with Sara goes unanswered. I just don't understand."

My father's voice, calm and mellow, comes from a bit farther away, maybe the back porch where Momma made him smoke. "Not everyone is going to parent the way you do, Connie."

"I know that." The slap of something hits the counter.

"Never said I didn't know that. But I'm not talking about good and bad parenting here. I'm talking about basic child welfare."

A snort, silence.

She spoke often enough about calling someone in, of mentioning it to someone in town, of asking questions. But Sara's momma would call then, out of the blue like Momma's blue moon, and for a while Momma would stop wondering.

We were in the kitchen, homework spread between us, when Momma got home one night. My father had come in thirty minutes before, boots caked with mud, a mumbled *ladies* trailing in his wake. Momma's greeting was louder. "You girls done yet? Want to help me start on dinner?"

"Sure," I said, bouncing up with a request of my own on the tip of my tongue.

She saw it, waved a hand at me, "Later."

It was over fried potatoes and fish, fresh dill and lemon, green salad in a shallow bowl, that I asked, "Momma, could I have dinner at Sara's house Friday night?"

My parents exchanged a glance, Sara and I exchanged a look.

"Friday?" Momma said it carefully, like the word might bite her tongue. My father shrugged, his acceptance of the date, and I turned unblinking eyes to her. "If all your homework is done and you're home around ten or so it shouldn't be a problem, Angie."

"Thanks!" I smiled, cheeks stretched to aching.

"What's your momma cooking?" This question was pointed at Sara, a barb from one housewife to another. Momma wanted to know if she was in danger of losing the girls in a meal competition.

Sara raised one shoulder, the thick glasses catching light

from the pendant above the table, the flash concealing her eyes. "I've been in charge of cooking when I'm home, so it'll probably be whatever Mrs. Simmons teaches us this week in Home Ec."

Momma smiled, the charming smile of a winner from the winner's circle crowned with carnations. "That sounds lovely. I hope you girls have a good time."

That was a Monday night and Sara spent the night as usual. In the morning we rode the school bus together, like we had most days since the third grade. I still only had a learner's permit, not that it mattered since we only had the one car. The rest of the week we went back and forth, talking about the girls in homeroom and the boys. We talked about the books we were reading and who smiled back at us in the library. We talked about nothing, the kind of nothing that seems really big when it's happening, the kind that takes up the whole world and buzzes in the back of your head while you sleep.

The evenings were a routine of homework, meals, and dishes. My parents treating her like the second child they'd had but somehow forgotten about until I'd pulled her inside one day to say *Momma, this is Sara*. But Thursday after school she paused after the bus dropped us off, hesitant.

"My momma wants me to come home tonight, you know, to make sure the house is ready for you tomorrow."

"You know I don't care." I snorted, tugging on the straps of my backpack to get them to lie flat. "I'm just excited to see your house. Didn't realize you had one. Thought maybe you lived under a toadstool or in a bird's nest."

"Yeah, well. You know mommas."

I snorted again, a habit that my own kept reminding me was an unladylike behavior. "Yep."

"I'll see you tomorrow, okay?"

"Sure," I said, waving and already walking away, wondering about dinner and if I could put off doing a paper for English due next week.

"Bye, Angie."

"See you later, Sara."

The next day I walked down the gravel road with her, a direction I hadn't taken since that winter we'd met in the woods. After that meeting she'd always seemed to find her way to me, I never had to go looking. We walked with the sun beating down and the sound of birds in trees, sweat-shirts tied around our waists.

I picked out her red mailbox first; you couldn't see the break in the trees that led to her house. Most of the places on the hill had these little winding drives that led back away from the main road, to cabins perched on the edge and looking out. The views weren't great, but they were better than nothing, and like my father said, on a clear day you could almost see the ocean. It was enough for most of us.

The red was faded, though, without numbers or name, just a rusted old box on a rotted stump sticking out of the earth. The drive looked overgrown and green, the under-brush growing right up close and tall weeds growing down the center.

"Nobody drive at your house?" I asked, knowing a car would have kept the taller weeds from growing, knowing that someone at some point would have complained about all the branches reaching out to scratch paint.

"Not much anymore," Sara said. "Car hasn't run for a while now."

"That's too bad." I didn't know what else to say. The idea of her not having a car to get around in made me uncom-fortable and a hot flush crept across my cheeks. I knew there were things she didn't have, things that my parents bought in duplicate on the sale rack or stuck seconds of into the shopping cart; packages of white socks and underwear, the kinds of shirts that faded the more you washed them and shoes with soles that lasted just the season.

In my mind I saw my momma handing Sara a white plastic bag a million times, the image of Sara growing and changing. The pink glasses were a constant, not because they aged with her, but because state insurance paid for a new pair every year.

I glanced at her, caught her watching me. "It's okay," she laughed. "I don't mind not having a car."

I shrugged, "I know. I just wish you did."

She lifted one shoulder, "It'll happen eventually. Gotta pass a driver's test first."

I groaned. "I can't parallel park. Is that even a thing? I've never in my life seen anywhere you'd have to park like that."

"There are spots like that down around the courthouse."

"I don't believe you."

She laughed, "No, really. I swear, like, you know, all around the building."

"Well I think it's stupid. And a waste of space. Who the hell needs to know how to park like a dumbass to pass a driver's test?"

"Other dumbasses?"

I was still laughing when I saw the house. I say saw, saw like I looked at it with my own two eyes, like my eyes were actually in my head and attached and sending these sight-seeing messages to my brain. But what my eyes saw wasn't what was really there. I don't think so, at any rate. I think what was there had been dressed up for my arrival.

A white house, the kind seen on the plains surrounded by farmland, glimpsed between two gentle hills, with two stories and two dormered windows. A deep front porch covered the first story, two wide steps leading up, and in the shaded space an open front door. Everything about it came in pairs, the windows on either side of the door, the shutters, even the potted plants on the steps.

I stood, mouth hanging open, knowing that the house was weatherworn and not that bright fresh white, knowing that the glass in the windows was gone. There were no shutters, not black and shiny, there were no potted plants. My head ached, trying to see what was there and what wasn't. I shut one eye, squinting through the sun. I could see it then, the way it was, an abandoned house in shoulder-high weeds on a small rise, a tree growing through the boards of the front porch.

I felt Sara take my hand, felt how warm she was, knew I was cold.

"Give it a chance?"

I nodded.

I kept both eyes open as we walked up the paved path. Curtains were pulled across the windows, heavy velvet backs dark to keep out the sunlight. They were bleached just enough, and my lids fluttered, my right almost closing as I squinted.

Then I saw movement beyond the glass of the front door, a shadow coming up from the back of the house. If I squinted I would see it, I would see something that was not the woman coming into view. Her hair was blonde like Sara's, cut short and even with her chin. She pushed the door open with an elbow, whipping her hands on the apron around her waist.

"I was just doing some washing up." The woman smiled at Sara, turned her head slightly and smiled at me.

"Angie, this is my momma; Momma, this is Angie."

I held out a hand. "Pleased to meet you, Mrs. Covert."

Her smile widened. "It's a pleasure to meet you as well, Angie."

I smiled, smiled like I had in the fourth grade and I'd lost first place in the spelling bee. I froze it on my face, keeping it there and as open and honest as possible to hide the heart stopping fear lurking just beneath. She was going to touch me, the shadow come out of the house to stand in the shade of the porch. I felt sunlight on my back and looked down, wondering if Sara's momma stood in it. No, she remained in shade, the tips of her plain shoes right up against the line between light and dark.

Her hand in mine was cool, firm, and she gripped it just enough to let me know she was there. No more pressure than that, no less.

"Come on in, girls." Mrs. Covert stood aside, using her back to keep the screen door open.

From the open front door a straight hall led back to the kitchen and the rectangle of the back door. An arch to the right opened on the living room and a set of stairs went up on the left. The cool interior buzzed with electric fans and the swish of the air conditioner coming on. A radio played low in the kitchen, too low to catch the tune.

"Wanna see my room?" Sara took the first two steps up, moving ahead of me, but paused, glancing back.

I snorted, "Of course!"

I climbed the stairs, looking down, watching Mrs. Covert through the banisters as she passed down the hall and toward the back of the house. Her shape seemed to waver for a moment, and though I could see the fall of light from the open back door down the length of the hall, I could not see the woman's shadow.

There were only two rooms at the top of the house, the one on the right belonging to Sara. She pushed the door open and we went in. My eye twitched, tempted to close, to see the world through just one iris. I touched the lid, trying to calm the jump, and looked around.

"It's not much, but I'm glad you get to see it. I spend so much time at your house that I don't really get a chance to clean it up much for company."

I waved a hand, looking at the collage of photographs on the walls. "How many *National Geographics* did you cut up?"

Sara laughed, "About a million."

Her walls were a forest. Birds peeked out from every angle, the flat glossy paper showing deep Northeast woods dressed in moss and tropical rainforests. The room was a mass of green, vibrant breathing green, but everywhere the flash of bright plumage. Exotic birds in yellow, blue, red, and pink, species I had seen in textbooks and flipped past, looked back at me. Even her ceiling was covered, the door of her closet and the back of the bedroom door. I was overwhelmed, wondering if she might sleep somewhere else until I saw the thin twin mattress shoved into a corner. Green blankets and pillows, not plush or fresh like the magazine pages, but dusty and fading. But you didn't see the wear, not when your eye was drawn to so much else.

"Wow."

"I know." Sara lifted a shoulder. "It's a lot. Like, a lot a lot, and you probably think I'm a freak, but I love the woods. I wanted to bring them inside with me when I was little, and at first it just started out as one wall but it spread, you know?"

I nodded.

"And I hardly ever sleep here, and no one sees it. Well, now you've seen it."

"What are you talking about?"

She looked around, she looked at the sad bed on the

floor, looked through the pink plastic glasses at how she thought I must have been seeing her room. Her room in a house that wasn't really a house anymore, living with parents who were not living.

"It's a lot."

I laughed then, I laughed because it felt good. "I freaking *love* your room. I can't believe your mom let you do this. I wish my mom would! I mean, I wouldn't cover it in green stuff. But you know, like, travel stuff? It would be amazing!"

She smiled, just a bit, and I wanted to reach out to her. I wanted to take her hand, I wanted to squeeze her so I would know she was real, so I would know it really had been another little girl I'd met in the woods all those years ago, another little girl I gave my Ice Queen wand to. And the years between? If I could prove that one moment to be real, the rest would fall into place.

I didn't take her hand, but I met her gaze, her pale green eyes brightened by her surroundings. "I really, really like your room, Sara."

We went downstairs, talking and laughing, like it was my house, talking and laughing like I didn't half hear a door banging on hinges in another place, like I didn't feel cold on the back of my neck.

As we passed the living area I glanced into the dim room. A man sat with his back to us, illuminated by the blue glow of the nightly news. I wanted to ask, *is he there?* I wanted to know what Sara would say if I'd voiced it aloud. She'd seen it on my face, she knew.

Give it a chance, okay?

"Hey, Daddy!" Sara skipped into the room, throwing her arms around the man's shoulders.

"Hey, baby," he said, reaching up to pat her arm.

I could hear the smile in his voice. I heard that smile in

my bones. Instantly an image of my own father flashed in my mind, waiting on the back porch after school for him to come home and watching him come up the drive, seeing his face light up when he saw me. It was that smile, it was light-of-my-life kind of happiness, and tears pricked the corners of my eyes.

The man turned, grinning, to face me. "Who might this be?"

Sara extended a hand toward me. "Daddy, this is Angie; Angie, this is Daddy."

I held out my hand, stepping forward. "Pleased to meet you, Mr. Covert."

"Likewise, young lady." He shook my hand, tilting his head at me in a gallant fashion before turning back with a grin to his girl. "You two should go help your momma in the kitchen. I don't know what was going on, but I could've sworn I heard all the pots we own rattling."

I stepped back into the hall, looking toward the kitchen and the open back door. I could just see Mrs. Covert. She stood, motionless, waiting, her face a blank, arms limp at her sides.

"Pasta okay?" Sara asked, going past me and down the hall.

"Yeah, sounds great." I followed, watching Mr. Covert turn back to his news, the way his shoulders slumped.

"Come to help prep dinner, Momma," Sara said, sweeping into the kitchen. She pulled a large pot out of a cabinet and went to fill it at the sink.

"That's sweet of you."

I watched their dance, the easy way Sara took over and handled everything while at the same time Mrs. Covert seemed to be in charge. But it was Sara that opened cabinets and jars, Sara who stirred the sauce and set the table. Mrs.

Covert bustled, moving from place to place with objects. From the corner of my eye I saw her place forks, set out napkins, but when I looked at her head-on there was nothing in her hands and Sara was there, setting the table.

Dinner didn't take long. Time enough to boil pasta and heat up canned tomato sauce. Sara went to let her daddy know dinner was ready, and he followed with an easy stride. He talked about what had been on the news, asking his wife her thoughts, wondering what Sara had to say. I watched them, chewing, silent. Once or twice Mr. Covert asked me what I thought about what was going on in the world.

"I honestly don't pay attention."

He shook his head, "You should. It's your turn next. Soon you girls will be driving and then voting. Might as well know a little bit about the world before you jump right in."

I nodded, forking another bite up so I wouldn't have to speak. My parents asked me things, like, had I done my homework or what happened at school or if I'd thought any more about a summer job. If they'd asked me, any of them, what the touring schedule of my favorite band was or what the name of the nail polish I was wearing was called, I could've said. But the world beyond the road I lived on seemed to be too far away to see clearly just yet.

"It'll come into focus all too soon." Mrs. Covert spoke, pulling my thoughts from the air between us. She smiled at me, soft and sweet. "Doesn't seem that long ago that Sara came running home going on a mile a minute about the new friend she'd made. I'm glad you've been there for our girl."

I nodded, looking down. Sara's foot nudged mine under the table.

Sara and I washed dishes by hand at the sink. It went quickly, with only two of everything to clean, and no matter how I tried to remember the meal we'd just shared I knew the Coverts had and hadn't eaten. In my mind I could clearly see loaded forks going to their mouths, hear the scrape of the tines on plates. But with everything washed up the draining rack stood only half full.

Two cups. Two plates. Two forks.

"What time is it?" I looked around, searching for a clock.

Sara went to the window, pulling the lace curtain aside to peer outside. The sun had set but there was still that faint wash of light, just enough to see the trees and shadows by. "Looks about 8:30 or so. Thank goodness summer break is almost here."

"Right? I'm so ready. I think I'm going to apply for that fast food job if you do. I bet we could get the same shift if we told the manager we share a car."

"Think so?"

I nodded, "Yeah. I better go, though."

We walked down the hall, the living room dark, the top of the stairs silent. I didn't know where Mr. and Mrs. Covert had wandered away to, if they were waiting in the wings somewhere to tuck Sara in, to kiss her goodnight.

I paused on the front porch, crickets humming, and listening for the non-sounds of the inhabited house behind me; silent, like silent nights and silent cemeteries, silent like last rights and the hopeful fast-paced heart of the hunted.

Sara took my hand, squeezed it tight. "Thanks for coming tonight."

"Of course," I laugh snorted, wrinkling my face at her in an expression meant to convey the stupidity of her feeling the need to thank me because *of course* I would have come. Always.

She laughed, "No, really, Angie, be serious for just a

minute. Thanks for being here tonight." Sara paused. "I love them."

And she did, I knew it like I knew my parents loved me, I knew it like I knew those ghosts loved her. I smiled. "Thank you for the invitation. And I really do love your room."

"Maybe we'll have to start saving magazines and do yours next."

"Maybe, yeah."

We smiled at each other, those big dumb grins you get when you don't need words to tell the person in front of you that you love them. The big dumb grins that come along when all is right with the world.

"I gotta go." I took a step away, looking up at the sky through the trees. "Momma said nine."

"Sure you don't want a flashlight or some company?"

I shook my head, turning way and starting down the drive. "It's okay. It's a short walk and it's a nice night."

"See you later, Angie."

And I could not tell if it were Sara or her momma or her daddy who spoke. I walked, feeling the three of them at my back, looking up to see all the stars that I could see. They were coming out, not one by one, but in great fat brush strokes that lit up the night.

ACKNOWLEDGMENTS

There have been several writing groups over the years, each one going over pages and reading outlines and listening to ideas. The Plotholes came first and more recently The Firestarters. I'm thankful for each of you and the endless hours spent reading. I wouldn't have gotten as far as I have without your support and willingness to reread pages.

I'm thankful for the boundless support from all my friends and family - you know who you are. I'm afraid I would forget someone if I listed you all and I'd lay awake at night worrying I'd made an unforgivable mistake. Then I'd end up haunting someone after I died, trying to make it up and apologizing endlessly. What might seem really small, texting to say hello or sharing a meme or some random fact, those are the things that mean more than you know. Thank you for being here with me.

For all the writing I haven't gotten done I have to thank Graham and Sloan. But also, thank you my beautiful babies for all the joy that fills our days, the excitement and laugher, and the sad things too. You are the best parts of my heart and soul.

And Darrell, just so you know, and this is final and in writing - I love you more.

ABOUT THE AUTHOR

Kathryn Trattner has loved fairy tales, folk stories, and mythology all of her life. Her hands down favorites have always been East of the Sun, West of the Moon and the story of Persephone and Hades. When not writing or reading she's traveling as much as possible and taking thousands of photos that probably won't get edited later. She lives in Oklahoma with her wonderful partner, two very busy children, one of the friendliest dogs ever, and an extremely grumpy cat who doesn't like anyone at all.

Sign up for updates about new releases and get the exclusive short story *Fire Watch* at kathryn.substack.com

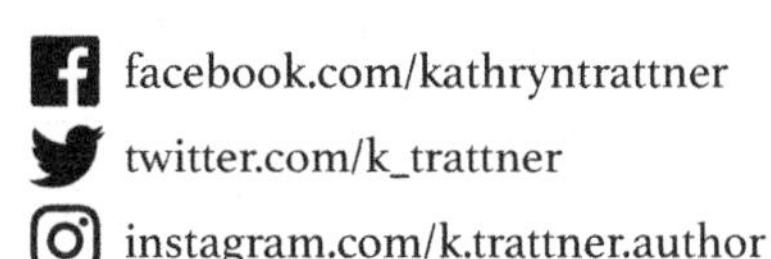

ALSO BY KATHRYN TRATTNER

Mistress of Death

Love. Death. Revenge.

Gabriel Mercer knows everything can be had for the right price. Raised in the shadow of the most famous assassin the city has ever known, she wants nothing more than to make a name for herself. Taking a solo contract from an up and coming politician seems like the easiest way to make it happen. But the contract comes with strings and soon Gabriel finds herself tangled in a web she won't be able to escape on her own.

Matthew Smith, a police officer rising in the ranks with a spotless record, discovers Gabriel at her lowest point; wounded and stranded on the wrong side of the river. He's drawn to her, unable to get past the uneasy feeling of familiarity, and saves her life against his better judgment.

As the web tightens Gabriel turns to Matthew for help. Their simple bargain, a life for a life, becomes harder to keep as their attraction grows. Soon Matthew realizes he won't be able to uphold his end of the deal. He isn't going to be able to let her go.

When the city begins to burn Gabriel will have to decide if she'll risk everything she's gained for a chance at revenge. Even if it means her future going up in smoke.

The Scent of Leaves

Janet has always dreamed about leaving her small town behind and starting over somewhere fresh. The only thing keeping her going in a photography obsession and her film camera. For her, life is a series of late nights spent working at a local gas station and days earning a final college credit before graduation. But she's been putting it off for so long she's starting to feel like it might not happen.

One night Tom appears, charming and handsome, and going out of his way to get to know her. Suddenly he's everywhere in her small town, appearing and disappearing at odd moments, creeping in on her days and nights. As they spend time together, Janet falling more under his spell each day, she begins to realize that reality is different around Tom. Small things begin to happen, odd occurrences turning into strange events, as Janet is pulled deeper into the mystery surrounding him.

In this modern retelling of the classic Ballad of Tam Lin the world is brought into sharp focus through the lens of a camera. The line between what is real and is not real blurs, nature stealing in around the edges, and Janet comes to understand that there is more at stake than just a broken heart.

Made in the USA
Coppell, TX
28 July 2021

59618436R00046